Pick a Powerpuff Path

the mayor's birthday surprise

by Heather Johnson

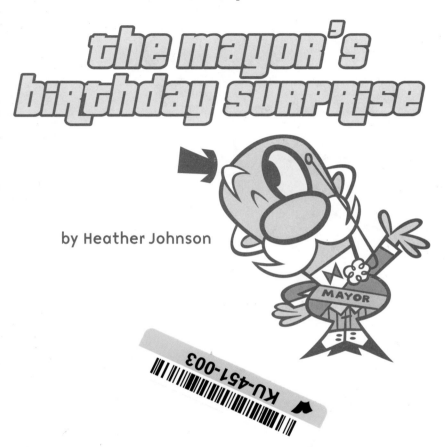

MAYOR

Scholastic Inc.
New York • Toronto • London • Auckland • Sydney
Mexico City • New Delhi • Hong Kong • Buenos Aires

ISBN 0-439-33230-3

Cover and interior illustrations by Mark Christiansen

Inked by John Hom and Philip Hom

Designed by Mark Neston

12 11 10 9 8 7 6 5 4 3 2 1   2 3 4 5 6 7/0

Printed in the U.S.A.

First Scholastic printing, February 2002

Read This First!

Sugar...Spice...and Everything Nice...

These were the ingredients chosen to create the perfect little girls. But Professor Utonium accidentally added an extra ingredient to the concoction—Chemical X!

And thus, The Powerpuff Girls were born! Using their ultra superpowers, Blossom, Bubbles, and Buttercup have dedicated their lives to fighting crime and the forces of evil!

The Powerpuff Girls live in Townsville, where they take care of the criminals, bad guys, and monsters that threaten the citizens of their beloved town. While they may be the best superheroes in town, there are lots of adults they count on, too. In every Pick a Powerpuff Path, you'll take on the role of one of the characters and help save the day.

In this adventure, you'll be the Mayor of Townsville. What the Mayor lacks in smarts, he makes up for in enthusiasm and his love for The Powerpuff Girls. And he must have some smarts, because he hired the beautiful and brainy Ms. Bellum as his assistant. In this story, the Mayor decides he wants to bake a birthday cake for the Girls and surprise them, using the very same cake recipe that his grandmother always used when the Mayor was just a boy. But nothing is ever simple for the Mayor, and he needs your help to make it happen.

continued...

The story will be different depending on the choices you make. Follow the directions to see how your story turns out. When you're done, you can start over and make new choices and read a completely different story.

So start reading—and choosing. The Mayor's got a cake to bake!

The city of Townsville! If there's one day the citizens like more than Saturday, when no one has to work, it's Friday, the day right before they don't have to work. Today is Friday. And the citizens are eager for the weekend to get here.

This included the Mayor, of course, who sat in his office working on very important city business: He was staring out the window. He couldn't wait to go home for the weekend. It had been a long, hard week, and he needed to relax.

But first...oh, no! A monster is attacking Townsville!

Ms. Bellum ran in to the Mayor's office and told him to make the call.

The Mayor got The Powerpuff Girls on the hotline—the special phone he used to call the Girls—just before the monster reached into the office window and grabbed Ms. Bellum and him!

"Oh, Powerpuff Girls!" the Mayor cried out as the monster pulled him away from the phone. "HELP!"

Blossom heard the cry, and she and her sisters, Buttercup and Bubbles, flew right over to save the Mayor and Ms. Bellum. In no time at all, they had that monster wrapped up in its own tail, crying for its mommy. Once again, the day was saved in Townsville, just in time for the weekend!

The Mayor was so happy he skipped home and tried to think up a way to really thank the Girls for always saving Townsville—they sure made his job easier! He thought all night with no success. But in the morning, he remembered that today, Saturday, was their birthday, and so he decided to bake a cake for them using his grandmother's very old cake recipe. It was the very same recipe that she had used to make the Mayor's birthday cakes way back when he was a boy, way back before he was a grown-up and the Mayor.

"Here's the recipe," the Mayor said to himself. "Let's see, flour...milk...butter...sugar...SUGAR! I don't have any!"

Oh, no! The Mayor can't make the cake without sugar! What will he do?

"Help!" the Mayor cried out from his kitchen. "Somebody help me!"

If the Mayor calls The Powerpuff Girls on the hotline to ask them for help, turn to page 8.

If the Mayor asks his assistant, Ms. Bellum, for help, turn to page 10. ✗

If the Mayor decides to go ask the Professor for help, turn to page 22.

Not having sugar was a problem, so the Mayor did what he always did when he had a problem: He called The Powerpuff Girls! Just as Blossom picked up the hotline, the Mayor remembered that he couldn't tell the girls why he was calling—he would ruin their birthday surprise!

"Oh, um, hi, Blossom," the Mayor stammered. "Um..."

"What's the trouble, Mayor?" Blossom asked. "We're on the case!"

"Um, well, see..." The Mayor could not tell her about the sugar, because then he'd have to tell her about the cake.

"Mayor?" repeated Blossom.

"Um, well, um, I forgot why I called you!" The Mayor was sweating bullets trying not to blurt everything out.

"Well, then, why don't you call us back when you remember," said Blossom, hanging up the hotline. She was a little annoyed, but she knew that sometimes the Mayor could be forgetful. She could tell he wasn't really in danger, though, so she wasn't worried.

Phew, thought the Mayor. *That was close! But now what?*

If the Mayor decides to try to find sugar on his own, turn to page 14.

If the Mayor decides to ask Ms. Bellum for help, turn to page 10.

If the Mayor decides to go ask the Professor for help instead, turn to page 22.

"Oh, Ms. Bellum! Ms. Bell-um!" The Mayor called out for his dutiful assistant several times before realizing he was not at the office, and she was not at his house!

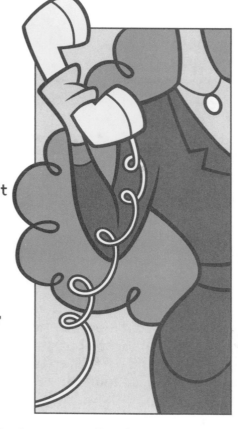

Oh, right, thought the Mayor. *It's Saturday!* He quickly picked up the phone and called her at home.

"Ms. Bellum, I'd like you to come over right away."

"Now?" sighed Ms. Bellum. "But it's Saturday. I don't work on Saturdays!"

"But I need your help, Ms. Bellum! I'm trying to bake a cake! And I need sugar!" the Mayor said anxiously.

"Sorry, Mayor, but I'm busy cleaning my pool," Ms. Bellum replied. And before he could explain more, she hung up the phone. The Mayor hung up the phone, too, and sighed with disappointment.

Looks like the Mayor won't get any help or any sugar from Ms. Bellum today! Now what will he do?

Suddenly, the Mayor's phone rang.

"Oh, I'm sorry, Mayor," said Ms. Bellum when he answered. "I dropped the phone before. I didn't mean to hang up on you. I'd love to help you make a cake!"

"Oh, Ms. Bellum, that's great," gushed the Mayor. "Because it's The Powerpuff Girls' birthday and this is the cake my grandmother used to make me, and it's going to be splendiferous! All I need is some sugar and everything will be all set!"

"For The Powerpuff Girls? Even better," said Ms. Bellum.

Was that an evil laugh the Mayor heard? *That's not how Ms. Bellum laughs*, thought the Mayor.

"I'll be right over," cackled Ms. Bellum, whose voice definitely sounded a little strange.

"And I'll bring you lots of sugar..."

The Mayor was very happy that Ms. Bellum had agreed to come over, but something seemed fishy. He wondered why she would say she couldn't come over, and then call right back and say she *could* come after all. *Why did she keep laughing an evil laugh like that? Oh, what should I do?* thought the Mayor.

If the Mayor suspects trouble and tells Ms. Bellum not to come after all, turn to page 18.

If the Mayor tells Ms. Bellum to come over anyway, turn to page 12.

The Mayor decided
not to worry about Ms. Bellum's strange behavior.
After all, she *had* agreed to help him bake the
cake.

"Thanks, Ms. Bellum. I can't wait to see you!"
the Mayor said into the phone.

Ding dong!

"Why, hello, Ms. Bellum!" said the Mayor,
answering the doorbell. It had only been a minute
since he had hung up the phone. "That sure was
fast!"

There stood Ms. Bellum, holding a huge bag of sugar. "Okay, Mayor, you make the cake," Ms. Bellum said excitedly, "while I work on another special surprise for the Girls!"

Ms. Bellum pushed the Mayor into the kitchen while she busied herself in his living room, building a huge steel trap.

Why does Ms. Bellum want to build a huge steel trap in the Mayor's living room? That doesn't seem like a very good birthday surprise!

Just as the cake was cooling, the Mayor walked into the living room and saw the trap that Ms. Bellum was building.

Hmm, thought the Mayor. *This doesn't seem right.* Just then, he saw a little black curl peeking out from under Ms. Bellum's red hair. *The red hair must be a wig*, the Mayor realized. This wasn't Ms. Bellum after all—it was the snaky-haired villainess Sedusa, *disguised* as Ms. Bellum! He'd been tricked!

The Mayor ran back into the kitchen and picked up the phone. Who should he call, though? If he called the Girls, that would ruin the birthday surprise; after all, the cake was almost ready. But what would happen if he called the real Ms. Bellum and she met the fake Ms. Bellum?

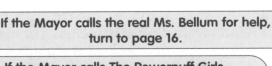

If the Mayor calls the real Ms. Bellum for help, turn to page 16.

If the Mayor calls The Powerpuff Girls for help, turn to page 40.

The Mayor decided that he didn't need anyone to help him; he could go buy some sugar at the supermarket. At least, he *thought* he could—but he'd never been shopping all by himself before! First, he went outside to wait for his limousine, but then he remembered that it was in the shop. So the Mayor got into his car and sat and thought about where the store might be. Finally, he remembered that he had attended the grand opening of a new supermarket just yesterday morning. After driving around for a while, he finally found it, right under a huge banner in downtown Townsville that read, GRAND OPENING—TOWNSVILLE SUPERMARKET.

"Hmm, this is a great idea," the Mayor said to himself as he entered the store. "All the food you could ever need, all under one roof! *Fantastic.*"

The Mayor was so awed by the supermarket that he decided to walk up and down every single aisle. "Oh, look," he said to himself. "Ketchup! And oranges. And pickles! All the pickles I could ever eat!" Finally, he got to the baking-supply aisle, which is where the sugar was located. Standing in the middle of the aisle was Mojo Jojo, Townsville's resident evil supergenius monkey!

The Mayor was so surprised to see Mojo that he just stopped in his tracks.

"Oh, hello, Mayor," said Mojo Jojo. "What are you doing here today? As for me, I'm buying cake mix, trying to find a suitable mix for me to buy that I can take home and make into a yummy cake. But I can't decide between a chocolate swirl or a banana nut cake...."

14

The Mayor interrupted Mojo Jojo and screamed, "Help! It's Mojo Jojo!"

This made Mojo Jojo angry. After all, he was just there to do his shopping, like any other Townsville resident. He was not breaking any laws. Why should he be hassled when he was just trying to buy some cake mix? Why was the Mayor screaming like that? "Stop shrieking!" demanded Mojo Jojo. "I can't stand it! Can't a monkey just shop in peace once in a while?"

If the Mayor decides to keep shrieking, turn to page 20.

If the Mayor decides to apologize to Mojo for shrieking, turn to page 39.

"Ms. Bellum, help!" cried the Mayor. "Sedusa was trying to help me make a cake! I thought she was you! She's built a..."

But before the Mayor could finish, Sedusa-as-Ms. Bellum stormed into the kitchen and hung up the phone. "So, you finally figured it out, Mayor," she said with a menacing chuckle. The Mayor shrieked and ran.

"You're pretty fast for an old Mayor," huffed Sedusa as she chased him through the dining room.

"It's all the exercise I get at the office," said the Mayor as he ran into the living room.

Finally, Sedusa stopped chasing the Mayor, ran into the kitchen, and picked up the finished cake. "Oh, Mayor," she purred. "Let's stop this silly game of tag and call the Girls over for their surprise!" She paused. "And if you don't call the Girls," she said, not so sweetly now, "I will destroy your priceless porcelain figurine collection."

The Mayor was stunned by this threat and stopped running. He thought he might cry. The Mayor loved his porcelain figurine collection!

Just then, the real Ms. Bellum burst in. "We're going to call the Girls, Sedusa, but your evil plan is *over.*" Ms. Bellum grabbed the cake, placed it safely on the kitchen counter, and then pushed Sedusa into the steel trap the villainess had obviously been building for the Girls. The Mayor quickly slammed the door of the trap shut and locked it.

"What a great team we make, Ms. Bellum!" he said, beaming.

"Whatever you say, Mayor. Just call the Girls, will you?" Ms. Bellum replied patiently.

The Mayor grabbed the hotline. "Oh, Girls! Please come over to my house! I have a surprise for you," the Mayor said.

The girls didn't know what was going on, but they flew right over. To their surprise, they found the Mayor, Ms. Bellum, and the evil Sedusa, who was caught in her own trap!

"Ms. Bellum, Mayor, what's going on here?" asked Blossom.

"You guys saved the day all by yourselves! Is that the surprise?" exclaimed Buttercup.

"Sedusa is not the only surprise," the Mayor said, smiling.

"I smell something yummy!" said Bubbles excitedly.

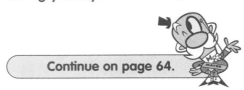

Continue on page 64.

"On second thought, no thanks, Ms. Bellum," said the Mayor. "You don't have to come over. But, um, thanks for calling back! And, by the way, I'm going out now, anyway."

The Mayor hung up the phone, but then wondered if he'd done the right thing.

Suddenly, the phone rang again! *I haven't answered the phone this much since the Townsville Phone-a-thon*, thought the Mayor.

"Mayor, it's me, Ms. Bellum," said Ms. Bellum.

"Again? What? Didn't we just hang up two seconds ago?" asked the Mayor.

"No, Mayor, that was at least fifteen minutes ago. But listen, I'm finished cleaning my pool, so it looks like I'll be able to come help you make that birthday cake after all! I'll be right over with the sugar," said Ms. Bellum.

"Are you sure you didn't just call?" asked the Mayor.

"No, Mayor! Why do you keep asking that?" asked Ms. Bellum. "In fact, my phone wasn't even working a minute ago."

"Okay, Ms. Bellum," said the Mayor, a little confused. "Why don't you come on over, then."

Ms. Bellum arrived with the sugar and she and the Mayor got to work mixing the cake. They followed the Mayor's grandmother's recipe perfectly. Just as they put the cake in the oven, the doorbell rang! It was another Ms. Bellum with the sugar.

"*Two* Ms. Bellums!" exclaimed the Mayor. "What a wonderful world this is!"

"No, Mayor," said the first Ms. Bellum. "There are not two of me. That is Sedusa trying to dress like me again. Can't you see that?" Sedusa was a snaky-haired villainess who had once kidnapped Ms. Bellum and then impersonated her.

"No, Mayor," said the second Ms. Bellum. "*I'm* the real Ms. Bellum and that is the impostor. Remember, you called me to come help and I called you back? In fact, we should probably lock that imposter up somewhere so she doesn't cause any more trouble!"

"No, Mayor, you called *me*," said Ms. Bellum #1, "and *I* called you back!"

The Mayor looked from Ms. Bellum #1 to Ms. Bellum #2 and back again. He was very confused. He had called Ms. Bellum today. That much he knew was true. But he had received *two* return phone calls. Each of the two Ms. Bellums must have called him back! But which one was the real Ms. Bellum?

If the Mayor picks Ms. Bellum #1, the one who helped him make the cake, turn to page 48.

If the Mayor picks Ms. Bellum #2, the one who arrived too late to help him make the cake, turn to page 54.

"That's very nice, Mojo. I'm glad you are just buying cake mix, but I'm going to keep shrieking," said the Mayor. "I just want to get my sugar, do my shopping, and get out of here before you do something evil."

"*Do something evil?*" repeated Mojo. "Why would you think I would be in the store to do something evil? I have no time for evil plans today! Today is Saturday, and I am at the market, and I am just trying to buy some cake mix!"

But the Mayor's suggestion intrigued Mojo Jojo. "Hmm," Mojo said to himself, "if the Mayor *thinks* I am here to do evil, then maybe I *should* do something evil! Maybe I should go ahead and hatch an evil plan! After all, the Mayor is already expecting it. But maybe that is no good. Maybe I should not hatch an evil plan when someone is already expecting me to, let alone the Mayor of Townsville. Oh, what do I care? He is just the dumb Mayor of Townsville. I am a supergenius villain!"

As Mojo stood there lost in thought, the Mayor stopped shrieking, grabbed the sugar, and left the baking-supply aisle. But Mojo, having decided to hatch an evil plan after all, followed the Mayor, who was wandering down the villainy-supply aisle by mistake. Mojo took lots of products, such as Salt That Looks Just Like Ordinary Sugar and Brussels Sprout Soda That Looks Just Like Ordinary Drinking Water, and put them in the Mayor's basket.

The Mayor suddenly noticed his basket was getting very heavy and caught Mojo putting villainous products into his basket! "What are you doing, Mojo? Are you doing something evil?"

"No, Mayor, I swear," pleaded Mojo in an innocent voice. "I am just trying to help. I just want to know what you are baking! I would like to know why you were in the baking aisle! I am not doing anything evil at all!"

Hmmm, thought the Mayor. *Maybe Mojo really is trying to help. After all, it's Saturday and even villains need a day off. On the other hand, this is Mojo Jojo!*

If the Mayor decides to apologize to Mojo for thinking he's up to evil, turn to page 39.

If the Mayor turns down Mojo's offer of help, turn to page 29.

21

"The Professor *must* have sugar," the Mayor said to himself. "Because I know that he made The Powerpuff Girls out of sugar, spice, and everything nice. I'm sure he has lots of sugar lying around for his experiments. He must have three-quarters of a cup of sugar that I can borrow to make my cake!"

The Mayor hurried to The Powerpuff Girls' house and rang the bell. Blossom answered in a flash.

"Hey, Mayor. What's up? What are you doing here?"

The Mayor was temporarily speechless. He couldn't tell Blossom the real reason he was there. "Oh, hi, B-Blossom," the Mayor stammered. "I'm just here to see the Professor."

Just then Bubbles flew over and greeted the Mayor. "Hi, Mayor! We're playing make-believe. Wanna join us?"

"Make-believe," said the Mayor happily, "that's my favorite game! Sometimes I even make believe I'm the Mayor of Townsville!"

"You *are* the Mayor of Townsville!" said Buttercup, joining her sisters at the door.

"Oh, yes...well, anyway, Girls, that sounds like fun, but I have a lot of business to attend to today," he said, thinking about the birthday cake he wanted to make for the Girls. He was very nervous that he was going to spoil the surprise.

"Please, Mayor," begged Bubbles. "Just for a little while?"

If the Mayor decides to play make-believe with the Girls, turn to page 26.

If the Mayor says, "No thanks," and heads right to the basement lab to talk to the Professor, turn to page 50.

The Mayor decided to run from the Girls so he could go home and bake their cake without telling them what he was up to. And so The Powerpuff Girls had no choice but to chase him, catch him, and take him to jail for shoplifting. It didn't matter that he was the Mayor of Townsville! He was caught leaving without paying for the sugar, and that was a crime!

At the Mayor's trial an hour later, the judge explained that there was a technical problem with the case. Because there was actually no shop, or Townsville Supermarket in this case, remaining at the time the Mayor took the sugar, he could not really be charged with shoplifting.

"What!" exclaimed Blossom. "That makes no sense!"

"Well, that's how the law was written," said the judge.

"Who would have written such a stupid law?" complained Buttercup.

The Girls looked at the Mayor, who was grinning sheepishly. Of course, he had written the law, and according to that law, he was innocent! So the Mayor grabbed the sugar and scooted out of there, thinking, *I must make this cake!*

The Powerpuff Girls were not very happy. Why was the Mayor acting so oddly? They decided to follow him. But where was the Mayor going?

If the Mayor heads home to make the cake as he'd planned, turn to page 56.

If the Mayor decides he likes the life of an outlaw and that he's going to continue with his life of crime, turn to page 32.

"Why, of course, Girls! I'm happy to play with you for a little while!" The Mayor walked into the house.

The Powerpuff Girls loved playing make-believe with the Mayor, because he did anything they told him to do. They all pretended to be TV Puppet Pals, then they all pretended to be international soccer stars. They pretended the Mayor was a Powerpuff Girl, and then they pretended each of the Girls was the Mayor of Townsville. Next, they pretended to be zookeepers and animals, teachers and students, train conductors and passengers. Hours went by. They played "pretend" so long that eventually they all got very tired.

Just as they all decided to stop for a snack, the Mayor panicked. He had forgotten about the sugar and his surprise for the Girls! He ran to the lab, where he found the Professor slumped over his desk.

"What's wrong, Professor?"

"Oh, Mayor, it's awful! I thought I had the formula for everlasting youth, health, brains, and instant popularity! But I didn't write it down and now I've forgotten it! That was hours ago. Oh, Mayor, I'm a mess. I'm just so upset!"

"Wow, Professor, that's too bad. But listen, there's something I'm upset about, too. Do you have any sugar I can borrow? I want to bake a cake and..." began the Mayor.

Continue on page 28.

"SUGAR? YOU WANT SUGAR?" The Professor glared at the Mayor. "I'm in the middle of a major scientific crisis, and you ask me for SUGAR? If you want sugar, then why don't you go to the supermarket and leave me ALONE!"

"But, Professor, I see sugar right there on your desk. Can't I just have a little? Maybe three-quarters of a cup?" asked the Mayor timidly.

"Please, just go," the Professor pleaded, and slumped over his desk again.

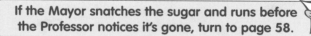

If the Mayor leaves the Professor and goes to the supermarket, turn to page 14.

If the Mayor snatches the sugar and runs before the Professor notices it's gone, turn to page 58.

"Mojo, you're *loco*," said the Mayor as he kept on walking. He wanted nothing to do with that meddling monkey! To think that Mojo Jojo was doing his shopping at the same place where all of Townsville had to shop! *That's outrageous*, thought the Mayor, vowing to make a law on Monday prohibiting all evil supergeniuses from shopping at the store. The Mayor took his cart to the checkout line, totally forgetting about the nasty things Mojo had put there, and paid for all the items.

Meanwhile, Mojo Jojo watched as the Mayor carried his shopping bags to the trunk of his car, and laughed an evil laugh. *I'm going to go home and watch the Mayor make this surprise cake,* thought Mojo, *and I will keep laughing and watching as the Mayor makes a cake that will taste terrible!*

Mojo Jojo sped to his secret lair inside Townsville Observatory to watch his monkey business unfold. He used his superpowered telescope that he always liked to use for just such occasions. With it, he was able to see directly into the Mayor's kitchen.

The Mayor, not knowing he was being watched, or that he had bought such villainous items as Salt That Looks Just Like Ordinary Sugar, whipped out his grandma's recipe. Mojo focused his telescope on the recipe and copied it down—it sounded like a really yummy cake, and maybe at some later time, when he wasn't always so busy with evil plots, he could try making a cake from scratch instead of from a mix.

Continue on page 30.

Unwittingly, the Mayor used the Salt That Looks Just Like Ordinary Sugar instead of sugar in the cake, which was just what Mojo Jojo wanted him to do.

Soon the cake was done, and the Mayor called the Girls on the hotline. "Oh, Girls," he said. "I have a surprise for you!"

They flew over right away to see what the surprise was.

"Happy birthday, Girls!" says the Mayor. "I've baked you a cake!"

The Girls giggled, and thanked the Mayor. But, suddenly, Bubbles started sniffing the air. "Mayor, I have a superpowered sweet tooth, and I can tell from here that the cake you made is not sweet! Something is wrong here!"

The Girls investigated and quickly discovered the evil product package in the trash can. "Where could you have gotten Salt That Looks Just Like Ordinary Sugar?" asked Blossom.

"I have no idea. Let's see, I was at the store, and I saw Mojo, and..."

"Mojo!" The Girls all said at once. They looked at one another and then out the Mayor's kitchen window. Using their super-vision, they saw right into the end of Mojo's telescope, where they saw Mojo Jojo spying on them. They zoomed over to Mojo's lair and captured the villainous monkey.

Meanwhile, the Mayor was wondering if his cake was really all that bad—after all, the Girls hadn't even tasted it yet! He took a small bite. "Oh, no! This tastes nasty! Bubbles was right!" he exclaimed.

He looked through his shopping bags, found the real sugar, and baked up a new cake while the Girls were depositing Mojo in jail for interfering in Official City Business (that is, ruining the Mayor's cake). The Girls flew back to the Mayor's house, just in time to see him take the new cake out of the oven.

Continue on page 64.

"Whoo-hoo! Freedom! Out of jail!" The Mayor felt free—truly free—like he'd never felt before. He decided he liked being a criminal—especially a criminal who couldn't be charged with a crime! He wondered what other crimes he could commit.

Meanwhile, the Girls still wanted to know what was wrong with the Mayor.

"Why is the Mayor acting so weird? Is he under a spell?" asked Bubbles.

"Maybe," said Buttercup. "Or he's Townsville's newest resident criminal! Let's keep an eye on him and see what he does, in case we need to stop him!"

"Let's go, Girls!" shouted Blossom, and the three Girls floated high above the Mayor as he wandered around town.

The Mayor decided to try belonging to a gang instead of being an outlaw all by himself. *Being a criminal can be lonely,* he thought, remembering how he used to work with Ms. Bellum. It seemed like that was only yesterday. That's because it *was* only yesterday that he had worked with Ms. Bellum.

First, the Mayor went down to the Townsville Dump and found the Gangreen Gang. "Can I join your gang?" asked the Mayor.

"Uh, beat it, old man," said Ace, seeing The Powerpuff Girls floating fifteen feet above the Mayor (who didn't know they were there). Ace couldn't figure out what was going on, but he wanted no part of it.

The Mayor went on to Morbucks Mansion, where the villainous little girl Princess Morbucks lived, and knocked on the giant front door. "Will you hire me?" he asked her.

"No way, José," said Princess, who noticed The Powerpuff Girls lurking at the end of her mile-long driveway.

I'm not José, thought the Mayor. *I'm the Mayor!*

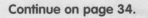

Continue on page 34.

Now the Mayor was getting desperate. He went to Townsville Park and found the Amoeba Boys standing on the grass. "Can I stand here with you?" asked the Mayor.

The Amoeba Boys saw The Powerpuff Girls right behind the Mayor and froze in terror. They wouldn't say a word to the Mayor.

Finally, with nowhere left to go, the Mayor's life of crime came to a sad end in an alleyway. "Crime stinks," he said to himself. The Mayor was so saddened by his new life that he cried himself to sleep on a bare patch of sidewalk.

Meanwhile, the Girls decided that even if they couldn't figure out why the Mayor was acting so strangely, they could at least take him home. They carried him to his house while he was still sleeping and tucked him in bed. On the way out, Blossom noticed the note the Mayor had written to himself that morning: MAKE THE POWERPUFF GIRLS A SURPRISE BIRTHDAY CAKE USING MY GRANDMA'S CAKE RECIPE. The Girls looked at one another and laughed.

"A cake? Isn't that nice," said Blossom.

"But it isn't even our—" Buttercup began, but was cut off by a fit of giggles from Bubbles.

"He's so cute," Bubbles laughed.

The Powerpuff Girls decided to make the cake themselves, while the Mayor was sleeping. Blossom and Bubbles got right to work, while Buttercup flew back to the remains of the supermarket and paid for the stolen sugar.

When the cake was done, the Mayor finally woke up. "How did I get here?" he wondered out loud as he walked out into his kitchen. But as soon as he saw the Girls there with the cake, he forgot his confusion and remembered his big plan for the day.

Continue on page 64.

"Um, no reason, Girls. I'm just surveying the damage to the supermarket. Making sure that everyone is okay. You know—very complicated Mayor's work. You Girls wouldn't understand." The Mayor did not want to give away his secret!

"So what do you need the sugar for?" asked Blossom.

"Sugar?" replied the Mayor. "What sugar? I don't know what you're talking about!"

The Mayor hid the sugar behind his back and sped off.

"Wait!" yelled Bubbles. "The Mayor stole that sugar!"

"Something is not right," said Blossom. "We'd better follow him!"

The Girls caught up to the Mayor and demanded that he return the sugar.

"I have no idea what you're talking about," insisted the Mayor. *Boy, these Girls sure make it hard to surprise them!* he thought.

"A criminal is a criminal, Girls," fumed Buttercup. "Let's get him and take him to jail!"

But the Mayor didn't want to go to jail—how would he bake the Girls a cake if he was in jail?

"No, please!" he begged. "Okay! I'll give back the sugar!"

If the Mayor confesses everything to the Girls, turn to page 44.

If the Mayor decides to run from the Girls instead, turn to page 24.

"I'm sorry for being suspicious, Mojo," the Mayor apologized. The Mayor decided to make it up to Mojo Jojo by babbling to the evil monkey all about his grandmother's cake recipe, and his plans to surprise The Powerpuff Girls for their birthday.

Mojo pretended to be interested in the cake recipe, but really he was trying to figure out how to mess up the Mayor's plan. Why did The Powerpuff Girls always get special treatment? Why didn't anyone ever bake a special cake for Mojo Jojo?

Mojo asked the Mayor lots of questions about the recipe and how to make the cake, and then finally he asked the Mayor if maybe he, Mojo Jojo, could come over to the Mayor's house and watch him make the cake, and maybe even help a little. "I have lots of baking tips I can share with you," offered Mojo.

Well, that's a very nice offer, thought the Mayor. On the other hand, could he really trust this monkey mastermind?

If the Mayor agrees to having Mojo come to his house to help bake the cake, turn to page 45.

If the Mayor turns down Mojo's offer to help bake the cake, turn to page 52.

The Mayor picked up the phone, dialed The Powerpuff Girls' number, and started to shout, "Girls, help! The evil Sedusa is in my house...." But before the Mayor could get all of this out, Sedusa grabbed the phone and put her hand over the Mayor's mouth.

"Girls, it's me," she said, sounding exactly like Ms. Bellum. "I'm at the Mayor's house and we have a little surprise for you, as a reward for all the hard work you do for Townsville and its citizens. You really should come over right away—the Mayor has worked awfully hard on it."

"Sure thing, Ms. Bellum," answered Blossom. "We're on our way!"

Sedusa hung up. "Okay, Mayor. Your precious little Girls will be here any minute. But first, you need to get into my trap."

The Mayor certainly didn't want to do that! He ran through the house, ducking under tables and running around things, which gave him an edge over the taller, larger Sedusa, who followed, trying in vain to catch the Mayor. But the Mayor lost a little ground every time he looked behind him, because he would get confused and think it was Ms. Bellum chasing him.

"Oh, Ms. Bellum, you don't have to chase me," the Mayor would say, stopping. But then he would remember that it was really Sedusa, and he would run away again.

After a few minutes the Girls burst through the door, looking for their surprise, but instead they found the Mayor and someone who looked like Ms. Bellum, out of breath and sweaty from all their running around. Black tresses were poking out of Sedusa's red wig, and the Girls soon realized what was going on.

"That's not Ms. Bellum, that's Sedusa!" the Girls shouted in unison.

"Looks like this trap is just your size," said Buttercup as she pushed Sedusa into the trap and Blossom slammed the door. The Mayor had tired Sedusa out with all the running around, so she had barely put up a fight with the Girls.

Meanwhile, the Mayor hurried into the kitchen and picked up the finished cake. "Happy birthday, Girls!" he said, smiling.

Continue on page 64.

41

"Everlasting youth, health, brains, and instant popularity!" said the Mayor. "Sign me up!"

The Mayor liked this idea very much and couldn't wait to drink the formula. He took a huge gulp and waited for the miracle. After a second, everything went all fuzzy, but then, suddenly, he felt so young—and alive! The Professor looked at the Mayor and jumped for joy. His formula worked!

"How do you like me now, Professor?" bragged the Mayor.

The Mayor rushed out of the Girls' house and into the world. He ran down to his office and passed lots of great, brilliant laws. He climbed the ladder of political success that he never even knew existed. Pretty soon he was no longer just Mayor of Townsville, he was King of Townsville. All his loyal Townsvillians—and villains—adored him. Even Ms. Bellum confessed that she had always doubted him, but now she couldn't believe how smart and great he was.

After about two hours of this, the Mayor remembered that he already had great plans for the day, and those plans included making a cake. He decided to go buy some sugar, go home, and make the cake. And while the cake was baking, the Mayor decided he would work on ways to end world hunger and create world peace.

Just as the cake was done baking, the Professor burst into the house with the Girls flying behind him. The Professor was shouting something, but the Mayor couldn't hear what he was saying—everything was getting all fuzzy again.

"I forgot to tell you, Mayor," cried the Professor. "The formula only lasts for two hours!"

The Mayor shook his head, and realized he was back to his old self. After another second, he'd forgotten all about his glorious afternoon and picked up the cake.

"Perfect timing, Girls," said the Mayor. "I was just about to call you."

Continue on page 64.

"Well, Girls, you see, this sugar is really for you," admitted the Mayor.

"Sugar?" asked Blossom. "Why would you give us sugar?"

"And why is it such a big deal?" sputtered Buttercup.

The Mayor decided to confess everything. "See, Girls, I was planning to use the sugar to make you a surprise birthday cake today, but since you know about it, it can't be a surprise. Mojo Jojo ruined my perfectly good plan. Anyway, now that you know about my plan, maybe you can help me!"

The Girls looked at one another and burst out laughing. "Sure, Mayor. We'd love to help!" They flew over to a stunned-looking cashier, paid her for the sugar, and then went to the Mayor's house to bake the cake.

"Okay, Girls," the Mayor said when it was all finished. "Thanks for your help, but now you have to play along. Close your eyes just like my grandma used to make me do when I was a boy. One, two, three..." counted the Mayor.

Continue on page 64.

"Okay, Mojo. I don't know why, but I think I'd love for you to come over and help me with my cake." *Maybe this could be the start of a new crime-defeating plan for Townsville*, thought the Mayor. Maybe he just had to get to know the villains in town a little better.

For his part, Mojo was plotting to secretly mess up the cake by putting all kinds of nasty things in it. But as he considered this plan, Mojo realized that he was too much of a perfectionist to go through with this plan. If Mojo was going to help the Mayor bake a cake, it was going to be the best-tasting cake ever! And it might be nice for once just to relax on a Saturday afternoon and not have to worry about dominating the world.

And so Mojo and the Mayor went to the Mayor's house. Mojo and the Mayor talked about cake mixes and batter while Mojo Jojo greased the pans. Suddenly, Mojo realized this was crazy. He, Mojo Jojo, Townsville's greatest supergenius villain, was playing baking games with the Mayor? It was totally nuts! Quickly, he decided to act.

First, he suggested that the Mayor go take a nap while the cake baked.

"I'll make the icing, Mayor," Mojo said. "You've done enough work already." Mojo would tell the Girls that he, Mojo Jojo, had made the cake all by himself and that it was his idea, not the Mayor's, to bake it in the first place! *Surely this would*

Continue on page 46.

45

confuse the Girls, he thought. Mojo Jojo was sure that if they thought he had made the cake, then they would not eat it, thinking something was wrong with it, and the stupid birthday surprise would be ruined!

"Maybe this is not the most villainous plan I've ever concocted," Mojo said to himself. "But it's not bad for a Saturday when all I wanted to do was go to the store and buy cake mix!"

So Mojo Jojo called the Girls on the hotline and told them to come over to the Mayor's house right away. "Come and eat some cake, Girls," he told them.

Blossom was very confused as she hung up the phone. "What can Mojo be up to?" she wondered.

"I don't know," said Buttercup. "But I do know that the three of us had better find out!"

The Powerpuff Girls zoomed over to the Mayor's house, where they found a snoring Mayor and a smiling Mojo holding out a cake. Could Mojo really be doing something nice for them? The cake sure looked good, though.

"Thanks so much for making us a cake, Mojo," giggled Bubbles. "It smells delicious."

"Yeah, Mojo," agreed Blossom. "This is so nice of you."

"I can't believe we have no reason to beat you up," grumbled Buttercup.

Mojo was shocked—and furious. The Girls actually believed that he had turned good? His plan was ruined. Ruined!

Just then, the Mayor woke up from his nap and came into the kitchen. "Oh, Mojo Jojo! My new friend! Where is the cake? And thanks for inviting the Girls over already!"

The Mayor didn't even notice that Mojo Jojo was purple with anger (maybe because it blended so nicely with the monkey's purple cape).

"It will take weeks to get my evil reputation back," muttered Mojo as he stormed out of the Mayor's house. "I will never work villainy on my day off ever again. That is where everything went bad, trying to work on my day off. I need a rest. No one can work every day of the week. We all need a break once in a while. I can't believe The Powerpuff Girls think I actually did a nice thing. Oh, how will I ever deal with this shame...."

Meanwhile, the Mayor decided it was time for the party!

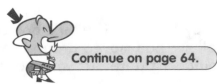

Continue on page 64.

"Ms. Bellum, I'd know the real you any- where," said the Mayor, pointing to Ms. Bellum #1. "You brought me the sugar for the cake first, just like the sweetie you are." Really, the Mayor was just guessing. Luckily, he was right.

"You're right, Mayor, but you know better than to call me sweetie or honey," warned the real Ms. Bellum, Ms. Bellum #1.

"No, Mayor, you picked the wrong Ms. Bellum," cried Ms. Bellum #2, who was really Sedusa.

Ms. Bellum #1 decided to take action. "We've been here before, you wacko," she told her nemesis. "I beat you once, and I can beat you again." Ms. Bellum got right to work taking care of Sedusa. Meanwhile, the Mayor called the Girls and asked for help.

By the time the Girls got there, both Ms. Bellums had moved around so much the Mayor couldn't figure out which one he'd picked as the real one. "One of the Ms. Bellums is really Sedusa. Help me, Girls! There's no time to be wrong!"

The Girls took no time to figure out who was who, and they helped Ms. Bellum finish defeating Sedusa.

"Oh, Girls, how did you know which one was which so fast?" asked the Mayor.

"Easy, Mayor," laughed Blossom. "Sedusa's hair is peeking out of her red wig. Plus, Ms. Bellum would *never* wear that much makeup. Her face looks great just the way it is!"

The Mayor was still confused, but he decided not to worry about it. Since the Girls were already there, he decided it was time for their party! He grabbed the cake. "Close your eyes, Girls!"

Continue on page 64

"No thanks, Girls!" said the Mayor. "I've got no time to play today. I'm on Official City Business, and I have to talk to the Professor immediately!"

Official City Business on a Saturday? Without Ms. Bellum? The Girls were disappointed that the Mayor wouldn't play with them, but mostly they were a little suspicious.

The Mayor ran down to the lab where the Professor was busy working. He asked if he could borrow some sugar, and started to explain his cake situation, but the Professor cut him off.

"That's it!" he shrieked. "SUGAR! Mayor, you've just helped me figure out the perfect formula for everlasting youth, health, brains, and instant

popularity!" The Professor poured all sorts of ingredients into a big jar, including sugar, and shook it up while the Mayor watched.

"Mayor, I want you to be my first guinea pig...er...I mean, taste tester!"

Everlasting youth, health, brains, and instant popularity? *Very tempting*, thought the Mayor. *Who could turn that down?* But all he had come for was sugar. He still had a cake to bake. Oh, what to do?

If the Mayor decides just to take some sugar while the Professor is preoccupied, turn to page 58.

If the Mayor decides to try the Professor's formula, turn to page 42.

"No, Mojo. I am the Mayor of Townsville and you are a villain. I'm afraid you just can't come over to my house."

"But, Mayor, what about this nice conversation we've had about cakes? Why do I always have to be the bad guy?" asked Mojo.

"Because you *are* the bad guy, Mojo. Too bad." And with that, the Mayor walked off to finish his shopping.

What? The Mayor of Townsville has dared to say no to Mojo Jojo? When all Mojo Jojo was doing was offering to help? Who does this Mayor think he is, anyway, Mojo wondered angrily. "I, Mojo Jojo, vow revenge on you, Mayor!" he announced to the empty aisle. And with that, Mojo went ape.

Mojo Jojo began wrecking the supermarket. If he destroyed the entire store, he reasoned, the Mayor couldn't buy what he needed for that stinking cake for those stupid little Girls! Since Mojo usually carried around a laser and other villainous tools, it didn't take very long for him to destroy every brick, every shelf, every tile, and every cash register in the whole store.

The Girls, who were out on superhero patrol, noticed the commotion, and flew down to find Mojo Jojo, his cape flowing in the wind, atop the pile of rubble that was once the Townsville Supermarket. His arms were in the air and he was victorious. And of course the Girls captured him right away and delivered him to a passing police car. Having finished with the evil monkey, they soon spotted the Mayor sneaking away from the rubble with a bag of sugar in his hands.

"Mayor!" said a surprised Blossom. "What are you doing here?"

If the Mayor ruins the surprise and tells the Girls the truth, turn to page 44.

If the Mayor lies and tries to continue on with his stolen sugar, despite the commotion, turn to page 36.

"Well, *you're* a fine Ms. Bellum, and *you're* a fine Ms. Bellum," said the Mayor to each woman. "But if I had to pick only one Ms. Bellum to be the real Ms. Bellum, then it would be *this* Ms. Bellum," he said, pointing to one of the Ms. Bellums at random. Unfortunately, he picked Ms. Bellum #2, who was really Sedusa in disguise!

Sedusa-as-Ms. Bellum got the Mayor to help her build a steel trap in his living room—telling him it was for Sedusa, but she actually planned to use it for catching The Powerpuff Girls. "Oh, brother," said the real Ms. Bellum as Sedusa and the Mayor locked her inside the trap. Her only consolation was that Sedusa would be inviting the Girls over in a few minutes (to put them in the trap, too), and then they'd straighten everything out.

Sedusa-as-Ms. Bellum ordered the Mayor to call the Girls to come get their surprise. The real Ms. Bellum told the Mayor to tell the Girls that Sedusa was in his house.

"Why would you want me to tell the Girls you're here?" the Mayor asked Ms. Bellum, whom he thought was really Sedusa.

"No, don't tell them!" barked Sedusa-as-Ms. Bellum. "Don't fall for that trick, Mayor. Don't tell the Girls that I'm—er—that *she's* here!"

The Mayor was confused. "If you really were Sedusa," he said, pointing to the real Ms. Bellum, "you *wouldn't* want me to tell the Girls, would you? But maybe that's what you want me to think, and so you're trying to trick me! But on the other hand—"He turned to Sedusa-as-Ms. Bellum. "If you

were *really* Ms. Bellum, you'd want me to tell the Girls that Sedusa is here, but maybe you don't want me to tell them because of another reason?!" The Mayor was thinking so hard that steam came out of his ears. "Oh, I give up!"

"Girls, come quick!" he said on the hotline. "I have a surprise for you, and I think you have to save the day."

Finally, the Mayor figured it out.

"I get it!" shrieked the Mayor. "*You* must be the real Ms. Bellum," he said to the real Ms. Bellum. "So that makes the *other* one Sedusa!"

Just then the Girls burst in, sized up the situation, and wasted no time freeing Ms. Bellum and putting Sedusa right in her very own trap. Sedusa barely had time to put up a fight.

All that thinking had made the Mayor very hungry. He grabbed the cake and said, "Oh, Girls, one more thing! Close your eyes..."

Continue on page 64.

Freed from the long arm of the law, the Mayor decided to run home, but he didn't realize the Girls were following him.

"What's gotten into the Mayor?" wondered Blossom as they flew along, high above the Mayor's head.

"Yeah, he's not acting very nice," said Bubbles.

"And he's definitely up to something," agreed Buttercup. "Why would he steal sugar?"

The Mayor got home and realized he'd had an awfully long day, what with his run-in with Mojo, his trial, and all. He decided he needed to take a little nap, and that he would make the Girls' cake when he woke up.

Meanwhile, the Girls had sneaked into his house so that they could continue to keep an eye on the Mayor. They found the cake recipe on a tattered and torn recipe card, along with the Mayor's to-do

list for the day, which did not include stealing sugar and going to jail! It included only one item: MAKE THE GIRLS A SURPRISE B-DAY CAKE USING MY GRANDMOTHER'S SECRET RECIPE THAT SHE USED TO MAKE ME A CAKE WHEN I WAS A BOY.

to do:

Make the Girls a surprise b-day cake using my grandmother's secret recipe that she used to make me a cake when I was a boy.

The Girls looked at one another and giggled. They decided to make the cake while the Mayor was napping. Bubbles and Blossom got right to work while Buttercup went back to the ruins of Townsville Supermarket to pay for the sugar.

When the Mayor woke up, he was still a little worn-out, but he smelled the delicious cake and saw the Girls in his house. He was a little confused, but also relieved that the cake was already made. "Hi, Girls," he said as he walked into the kitchen and picked up the cake. "Close your eyes..."

Continue on page 64.

"Boy, the Professor sure is in no mood to help me with my cake! But I'm sure he won't mind if I just take a little bit of this sugar and get on with my day!" said the Mayor to himself. The Mayor reached for the sugar, but in his hurry to get out of the Professor's way, he accidentally took the jar of Chemical X instead, which was sitting right next to the sugar!

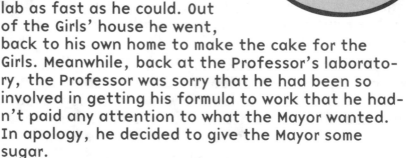

He rushed out of the lab as fast as he could. Out of the Girls' house he went, back to his own home to make the cake for the Girls. Meanwhile, back at the Professor's laboratory, the Professor was sorry that he had been so involved in getting his formula to work that he hadn't paid any attention to what the Mayor wanted. In apology, he decided to give the Mayor some sugar.

"Girls?" Professor Utonium called, hurrying out of the lab with a cup of sugar. "Would you bring this cup of sugar over to the Mayor's house? He's baking something and needs it for his recipe."

"Goody!" exclaimed Bubbles. "Maybe if we bring him the sugar, we can have some of whatever he's baking!" The Girls took the sugar from the Professor, and flew off to visit the Mayor.

By the time the Girls got to the Mayor's house, the Mayor had mixed up the cake (using Chemical X instead of sugar), put it in the oven, and was licking the bowl clean, just like he used to do when his grandmother made the cake. Suddenly, the Mayor slipped on some egg yolk he'd spilled on the floor. But instead of falling down, he found himself floating in the air instead! Thanks to the Chemical X in the cake batter he'd eaten, the Mayor had superpowers!

"Hey, I can fly! And I feel really strong, too!" the Mayor shouted. *Where did I get these powers from*, he wondered. And now that he had them, what should he do with them?

If the Mayor decides to use his new powers ▶ to cause trouble, turn to page 60.

If the Mayor decides to use his new powers to do good, turn to page 62.

59

As the Girls reached the Mayor's house, they heard the Mayor's voice coming through the kitchen window. He seemed to be talking to himself. They decided to fly up to the window and surprise him. But it was The Powerpuff Girls who were surprised when they looked inside and saw the Mayor floating above the kitchen floor!

"How did the Mayor get superpowers?" wondered Buttercup.

"I don't know," said Blossom. "But we'd better go tell the Professor about it. I don't think it's a very good idea to have a superpowered Mayor flying around...." And the three Girls sped back home, still carrying the cup of sugar.

The Mayor was still deciding what to do with his new powers. "Maybe I'll use my powers to take over Townsville! Oh, wait, I'm already the Mayor. Well, maybe I'll use my powers to take over a pickle factory! That way, I'll never run out of pickles!" The Mayor loved pickles, but he always had trouble opening the jars. But now that he had super-strength, that wouldn't be a problem anymore! The Mayor flew toward his front door, trying hard to hatch a plot to take over the world—or the world's pickle factories, anyway. But he'd never been very good at plotting— his decision to bake the Girls a cake was about as complicated a plan as he could manage—and he obviously even had trouble with that. By the time the Mayor got to his front door, the timer went off for the oven. The cake was ready! All of the Mayor's half-baked plans of world domination were forgotten in his rush to take the cake out of the oven.

Right after that, his doorbell rang!

He flew over to answer the door, holding the cake on a plate. It was The Powerpuff Girls, who canceled out the Chemical X inside the Mayor and the cake with one zap of their Antidote X ray gun.

Frankly, the Mayor was relieved. He never would have known what to do with those superpowers. It was way too much stress. Instead, he invited the Girls into his house for their birthday cake.

Continue on page 64.

My grandmother's cake is a miracle, thought the Mayor. *I can fly and I feel great! Maybe I'll become a crime fighter and give The Powerpuff Girls a vacation!*

The Mayor made plans to head out and start patrolling Townsville right away, but first, he remembered, he had to wait until the cake finished baking.

Just as the Mayor was finally ready to leave his house, thinking about all the good he planned to do and all the work he wanted to do with his superpowers to make the world a better place, the oven timer went off and the doorbell rang at the same time. He answered the door, holding the cake on a plate. It was The Powerpuff Girls!

"How did you know about my superpowers?" the Mayor asked as they zapped him with the Antidote X ray gun, canceling out the Chemical X inside him and the cake all at once.

"The Professor sent us over here to give you some sugar, but then we used our X-ray vision to watch you inside the house, silly!" said Bubbles. "So we went home to get you some antidote and then came back."

"Saving the world and doing good in Townsville is Girls' work," Blossom told the Mayor. "You just keep on baking cakes and leave the superpower stuff to us."

The Mayor quickly forgot all about fighting crime, and remembered his biggest plan of the day. He picked up his cake and smiled at the Girls.

Continue on page 64.

"Surprise, Girls!" shouted the Mayor, as the Girls looked at the freshly baked cake. "Here's an extra-special cake for your birthday, using the very same recipe my grandmother made for me when I was a little boy! It was the best cake ever!"

Blossom winked at Buttercup, while Bubbles giggled. "Thanks, Mayor," said Blossom. "We sure are *surprised*!" Buttercup laughed out loud, and then all three Girls got ready to chow down.

"I'm glad you're so happy," said the Mayor. "But why are you all laughing?"

"Well, there's just one thing," Blossom got out. "It's not *our* birthday, Mayor. It's *your* birthday!"

"Oh," said a very confused Mayor. "Well, I knew that it was *someone's* birthday! Happy birthday to me!"

They all laughed again and ate big slices of cake.

Once again, the day—and today, the cake—is saved! Thanks to, well, the Mayor! Happy birthday, Mayor!

THE END